Delicious English
CARAMEL TREE

www.carameltree.com

The Day
They Skipped
Emma's Birthday

CARAMEL TREE

Chapter 1
A Special Day

It was early in the morning and the house was quiet, but Emma was already awake. She was very excited. She was thinking about what the new, special day might bring. She was listening to all the sounds around her, hoping to hear something that she had been waiting for all night.

It was 5 o'clock in the morning, and everyone was still asleep. She pulled her warm blanket up to her chin and curled up in her bed. Her long, brown, wavy hair was spread across her yellow pillow. Emma couldn't hear anything except the gentle songs of the birds. She slowly fell asleep again.

Suddenly, there was a loud bang. It was the sound of her parents' bedroom door closing. Emma opened her eyes again and listened carefully. Her dad was going to the bathroom. In her mind, Emma counted the steps as he walked straight past her room. Then she heard her mom walking downstairs to the kitchen, where she turned on the coffee machine and started to make breakfast.

Emma counted up to twenty and then took a deep breath. Emma began to feel happy as she stretched under her blanket.

Today was a special day; it was her eleventh birthday. She was waiting for her parents to run into her room and shout "Happy Birthday!"

Emma pulled her blanket over her head and began to hum the birthday song. She sang the words in her mind, *'Happy Birthday to me, Happy Birthday to me, Happy Birthday dear Emma, Happy Birthday to me.'*

She held her breath and listened. She waited, and it became warmer under her blanket. When it finally got too warm, she pushed the blanket away.

'What is happening?' she thought. Her parents were doing their usual morning things even though this wasn't a normal morning.

'Today is my birthday!' Emma thought. *'Why isn't anyone coming to say Happy Birthday to me?'*

She could not wait any longer, so she jumped out of her bed. Without putting on her fluffy, pink slippers, she rushed to the door and pulled it open. She stood by the door for a moment waiting and listening, but she heard nothing.

Emma was confused.

Chapter 2
What Is Wrong?

Emma ran down the stairs. She dashed into the living room and stood by the entrance. She looked around in disbelief and wanted to cry. There were the bookshelves, the couch, the table, the sofa, the television, the fireplace, the cupboard, the radio, and the two green lamps, but there were no balloons, no 'Happy Birthday' sign, and NO PRESENTS!

'NO PRESENTS!' Emma was

disappointed.

    Behind her, Emma heard her dad coming

down the stairs. She waited for him to greet and say

'Happy Birthday' to her. However, he only said, "Good

morning, Emma." He didn't even see that Emma looked sad. Emma stood silently, not understanding what was happening.

'It's my birthday!' she shouted in her mind, but she didn't say it to her dad. She expected her parents to know it. She shouldn't need to tell them.

Mom walked out of the kitchen and looked at Emma.

"Good morning, Emma," she said with a smile. "Why don't you get dressed and join us for breakfast?" It was Saturday, and the family usually had a big breakfast on Saturdays.

"OK," was all that Emma could say. She felt sad that her parents did not remember her birthday.

Emma stared at her parents and clenched her fists. She was getting very angry. She turned around and rushed out of the kitchen.

As she was walking up the stairs, her older brother, Michael, came flying down and pushed her aside. He didn't even look at Emma.

"Hey, you," was all Michael said.

'What is going on?'
Emma thought bitterly and
ran up the stairs. She
slammed the bathroom
door behind her.

Then she washed her face and brushed her teeth, and the whole time she thought about why nobody remembered her birthday.

During breakfast, Emma didn't say a word even though her parents asked her many questions. Only Michael was talking excitedly about his soccer game.

"I am so thrilled," Michael said. "This is our first home game. Will you all come and watch?"

'You are excited?' Emma thought.
'It is my birthday, and all you can think about is a silly soccer game?'

After breakfast, Emma got up, took her dishes to the sink, and went to the garden without saying a word to anyone.

"What is wrong with her?" Michael asked after Emma had left the kitchen.

"I don't know," Dad replied. "Maybe she woke up too early."

Emma went into the garden and sat on the swing. She started swinging higher and higher, then suddenly stopped and jumped off the swing.

'That's it,' she thought to herself. 'They are planning a surprise party for me.' She smiled.

Emma danced her little happy dance and walked back into the house. She couldn't wait to find out what her parents were planning for her.

'*I love surprises,*' she thought.

'*I wonder what it will be!*'

Chapter 3

Spying

Emma walked casually into the kitchen and saw her mom washing the dishes. The breakfast was still on the kitchen table, and Emma started to clean the table and put all the food away.

"Thank you, Emma," Mom said. "How are you today?"

"Good," Emma replied. "What are you doing today?" she asked.

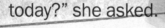

"I am taking Grandma shopping this morning, and in the afternoon, we are all going to watch Michael play soccer," Mom said.

'You won't have any time to prepare for my surprise birthday party then,' Emma thought. Her anger was slowly returning.

"Watching soccer is boring." Emma was annoyed, but she knew she had to go because she could not stay home alone. 'What a horrible way to spend my birthday,' she thought. Emma crossed her arms and walked out of the kitchen.

She walked through the house and searched for her dad. As she passed through the living room, she saw Michael playing a video game.

"Don't you have anything better to do?" Emma asked. "All you think about is playing games."

'Why aren't you planning for my birthday surprise?' Emma thought.

She wanted to say it out loud but she didn't.

"What is wrong with you, Emma? There's no school today, and there is nothing to worry about. Why are you so grumpy?" Michael shouted back. He didn't like it when he was disturbed while playing his favorite game.

Emma thought that maybe Dad was planning the surprise party. She heard a noise coming from the garage, so she went to check what it was. When she opened the garage door, she saw her dad working on his old car.

"What are you doing today?" Emma asked.

"I'm fixing my car, and then we are all going to

watch Michael's soccer game," he said.

'You won't have any time to prepare my birthday party,' Emma thought. Her anger was growing rapidly.

Emma turned around and walked back to her swing. She sat on it and began to think, 'Mom is going shopping with Grandma, Dad is fixing his old car, Michael is playing video games, and then we are all going to Michael's soccer game. So who is planning my birthday party?' She leaned back and looked up into the tree and had a scary thought.

'They forgot my birthday!'

Chapter 4
An Unhappy Afternoon

The day passed by quickly.

Everything happened as everybody had planned,

but not for Emma. She spent most of her day in her

room, playing with her dolls and reading books.

She drew a picture, but it wasn't a very nice one. She only used dark colors like brown, black, and gray; colors that represented her mood. Nobody called her on the phone, not even her best friend from school or her grandparents. Everybody had forgotten her birthday.

When it was time to leave for Michael's soccer match, Emma walked down the stairs and joined the rest of the family. When they reached the soccer field, the weather had changed and it began to rain. The wind blew cold air from the north, and Emma began to shiver.

Watching her brother play soccer was boring even though his team won, and he scored two goals. Emma felt miserable and wet.

On their way back to the car, Emma and her parents crossed the wet, slippery soccer field. Emma slipped and landed in a puddle of dirty, muddy water.

"Ahhhh!" Emma screamed angrily.

She stood up slowly. She was covered in mud.

Michael and his friends came running and began to laugh when they saw Emma. Emma felt even more miserable.

When the family finally arrived home, Emma ran upstairs into the bathroom. She had a hot shower and thought about the day and all the things that did not happen.

'No birthday party, no singing, no balloons, and

NO PRESENTS!' Emma thought. 'Only

soccer and mud! They all forgot about me. They

skipped my birthday! This was supposed to be a fun

day, the most fun day of the year, but all I got is mud.

Back at home that evening, Emma cleaned up and wore her pink robe. She was angry. Everyone had ignored her birthday, so she was going to ignore everyone. She walked passed Michael and pushed him aside.

"Hey!" Michael shouted. "What is wrong with you?"

"You!" Emma replied coldly and kept on walking.

She went into the kitchen, and Mom gave Emma hot chocolate and sandwiches. She sat down at the table and had the delicious snack without saying a

word to Mom. She didn't even say "Thank you!"

"How are you feeling now?" Mom asked, watching her quiet daughter.

"Mmmmmm," Emma replied with her mouth full as she left the kitchen without clearing the table. She saw her dad sitting in the living room and ignored him. She went straight up to her room without saying goodnight to anyone.

Once in her bedroom, she took off her robe and jumped onto her bed. She curled up under her blanket and started to cry.

'Nobody remembered my birthday. Nobody loves me,' she cried and slowly fell asleep.

Chapter 5

A Normal Day

The next morning, birds were singing again. Emma was awake, but this time she wasn't listening carefully. She didn't hear all the quiet footsteps that passed by her door. She didn't hear the sudden bang that echoed through the house, like the sound of an exploding balloon.

Suddenly, the door opened and Dad, Mom, and Michael jumped into her room. All of them were singing the 'Happy Birthday' song.

"Happy Birthday to you, Happy Birthday to you, Happy Birthday dear Emma, Happy Birthday to you!" They sang loudly and smiled at Emma.

Emma sat up in her bed and looked confused. She didn't understand what was happening. When she walked downstairs and saw all the banners, balloons, and ribbons, she slowly realized that today was her birthday, not yesterday! She smiled and danced her little happy dance.

"What was wrong with you yesterday?" Mom asked.

Emma looked deep into her mom's eyes and said, "Nothing, just a mistake I made."

'A mistake that ruined my whole day,' Emma thought.

Later that morning, Mom told Emma to put on her favorite dress because her friends were coming over for a birthday party. Emma was full of excitement as she thought of how the birthday party would be.

Emma started to imagine a beautiful party with nice snacks and lots of games to play. She imagined beautiful decorations and all her friends. She dreamed of the best birthday presents and all the fun things she would do.

'*Wait a minute,*' Emma thought, '*I already made a mistake like this yesterday by thinking about what should happen. I don't want to make the same mistake again today. I will just enjoy the day and not think about how the day should turn out.*'

With that thought, Emma learned not to have too many expectations. She knew that high expectations could only disappoint her if they didn't come true.